T0208413

A
SOUTHERN
DREAM

A
SOUTHERN
DREAM

DENSON JONES

To order additional copies of this book, contact:
Xlibris
1-888-795-4274
www.Xlibris.com
Orders@Xlibris.com
775113

As he rose from a deep sleep, he wiped his eyes and looked out the window to see the crops that he had helped plant months ago. The corn, tobacco and sugar cane, was growing just fine. He looked out over the estate and was proud of the acreage of land that his Massa had preserved to harvest those crops. He and his people had planted and harvested those crops that he was overseeing.

Jacob Jackson had come from a proud African tribe in his generation before he arrived on the Jackson Plantation in Laurel, Mississippi. His favorite pastime was fishing on the Mississippi River and reading from the Bible. Jacob would daydream all day about being free and he would let people know how he felt about the life he lived. He always stood up for righteousness and Godliness. He went to the neighborhood Baptist church every Sunday and even sung in the choir. He also loved to preach the word of God to anyone who would listen to him. He learned to speak English quickly and he had learned it faster than the other slaves.

Jacob was a God-fearing man and he lived a humble, solemn life. He lived with his wench, Sarah, and daydreamed of being the carriage driver of Johnathan Jackson Esquire, of the Jackson Plantation. He would dream of driving Mr. Jackson to town to get supplies and to attend other business matters. He also dreamed of driving the carriage and tending to the majestic horses that led that carriage. Some days Jacob would dream that the field slaves would talk down to him and call him all kinds of names like, Uncle Tom and Sambo. In Jacobs's eye, the other slaves were really jealous of his position and his title on the plantation. Even when he dreamed that he lived in a house on the side of the big house, they would call him a house nigger. And they would say that he sucked up to the Massa.

He was very verbal and spoke out about his position, but he would help his fellow slaves any way he could with food, water and clothing. After a hard day of work, Jacob would go down to the slave quarters and read the bible to the slaves while secretly teaching them how to read and write. It took a while for them to learn, but he was a very patient man. He had to be very careful with his teachings for in that day, it was against the law for Negros to read or write. But he did what he could do for his African brothers and sisters.

One day, Jacob came home from driving the team of horses back to the plantation after getting supplies for the Massa. He was putting the horses away when he heard a scuffling sound in the stable. After looking further into one of the horse stalls he saw a runaway slave from another plantation.

Sometimes slaves would run away and hide away on another plantation.

He abruptly approached the slave and asked him what he was doing hiding out in his Massa's horse stalls and what his plans were. The runaway slave told Jacob he wanted to find the Underground Railroad and go north.

He begged for mercy so Jacob would not tell the Massa or the overseer their secret. Jacob made the decision to help the runaway and brought him food, drinks and blankets for a couple of days until one-night, Jacob took him out of the stalls so they could meet a man that knew more about Harriet Tubman's Underground Railroad. The Underground Railroad was organized to help slaves escape North to freedom.

That night he said so long to the runaway and prayed that he had a safe and successful journey to the North. Jacob saw a lot of turmoil in his life on the Jackson plantation. He saw his own parents separated and sold to other plantation owners. He also seen his siblings sold off also like cattle. Slaves were most economical on large farms and plantations, where labor-intensive cash crops, such as tobacco, cotton and sugar Cain could be grown and be grown.

By the end of the American Revolution, slavery had proven unprofitable in the North and was dying out. Even in the South the institution was becoming less useful to farmers as tobacco prices fluctuated and began to drop. Then around the late 1700's, Cotton replaced tobacco as the South's main cash crop and slavery became profitable again.

 Jacob hated to see his fellow slaves, young and old, whipped and hung for just trying to escape the oppression of

slavery. He himself tasted the whip at the hands of the overseer one day just for eyeballing a White Women. Even though that was a long time ago, Jacob was glad that those days were in the past. This had happened way back in the past. Jacob never wanted those days to return to haunt his memories, but time and time again, occasionally, they would do just that. They would just return with a vengeance.

He hated those recurring memories, but try as he did, he could not stop them. Jacob liked to wipe the slave owner's carriage down and then ride off over the wide acreage of land in the cool of the day, with the sun on his face before putting the carriage away. As the master carriage driver, he would have loved the privileges his Massa would give him.

He would stay in the carriage house on the side of the big house and he would've had a pretty decent wardrobe, unlike his fellow field slaves, who wore withered and tethered dirty clothes. He would also eat the same food his Massa ate, plus leftovers. He would have a better life than most slaves. As Jacob was wiping down the carriage on this fine and lovely spring day, he couldn't help but wonder how the young slave, that he caught in the horse stall, was doing. He wanted to know if the runaway made it to the Underground Railroad. Jacob also wanted to know more about other runaway slaves trying to make it all the way up North. He often would sit under a sycamore tree and dream about running away with his wench Sarah.

Some days the Massa would let Jacob and Sarah take the carriage into town for a service checkup. Then on the way back to the plantation, they would stop for a short picnic in the pasture under one of those sycamore trees.

They loved doing things like that together. After the picnic they would just lay on the blanket and look up at the approaching evening sky and daydream about living free and raising a family up in the Northern States. This is what Jacob liked to dream about.

After their picnic they would gather their belongings and drive slowly back to their home on the Jackson Plantation. Sarah would go to their house and Jacob would care for the horses, and then further wipe down the carriage to get it ready for the next day.

After a long day, Jacob and Sarah would read from the good book, pray their nightly prayer for freedom and go to bed, hoping the whole night long that one day they would wake up to a different world and have a better life in the future.

They prayed for a future free from White oppression, violence and hatred. Jacob would daydream all day long about simple things as he drove around the countryside with his Massa. He saw all kinds of sights, good and bad, as he drove his Massa around. But he was really just a humble African that was made a slave, living in Mississippi in the 1800's.

Like many Africans, he learned to adapt to the White American way of life. Although he saw a lot of bad things happen to his fellow African made slaves, he could not stop the White overseer or the Massa from raping and impregnating the slave winches.

Even though he hated his life in the Americas he had to watch his fellow slaves running away and getting chased by slave catchers and run down by vicious dogs. He hated watching the slaves brought back to the plantation and beat and whipped for their transgressions. But time and time again this would happen all over Mississippi plantations. This treatment against the slaves was happening all over the South. No matter what slaves saw or did against the Whites, they still were not deterred by the whippings. Just like the Klu Klux Klan, the slaves had their own secret meetings and tried to stay united. They believed in the old adage, that there was strength in numbers.

The next morning, Jacob woke to the sounds of the slaves in the fields picking cotton and singing hymns from their African roots. He was powerful hungry as he wiped the crust from his sleepy eyes and washed up to eat breakfast. Sarah was already in the kitchen cooking up some grits, biscuits and bacon.

The morning smell of Sarah's breakfast cooking made him more hungry than usual. Jacob had just awakened from a deep sleep and he told Sarah, while eating breakfast, about his latest dream. He explained to her how they ran away one night and found the Underground Railroad and met Harriet Tubman in person. He went on to say that in his dream, their escape to the Northern States was a success.

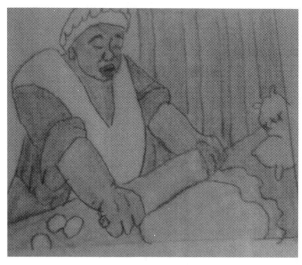 Jacob loved Sarah's cooking. He especially loved her biscuits from scratch with molasses on top. After breakfast, Jacob would do small chores around

the house and care for his wench. He would then go out and lie under the sycamore tree and dream about when he was back in Africa with his siblings, relatives and friends. He would lie under his famous tree until his Massa called him to work. Today was a day that he fretted about because there was a slave auction in town and he and his owner were going to it. His Massa wanted more slave women to breed.

He really hated those auctions because it reminded him when he first came to America and stood on the auction block himself. He had to watch other Africans become slaves and told about getting introduced to the slave master and the overseer that would rule with an iron hand. They would also learn about the whip fastened to the hip of the overseer.

It was going to be a lot that each slave had to learn, and one thing was to obey and not try to run away from being a slave. They would even have to exchange their African names for American White names. No slave wanted to exchange their real African name, for an

American White name. All Africans hated that situation that they were put in. But if they resisted, they would be tied to a tree or a stake and whipped, until they gave in. Most of the African men resisted until they could no longer take the pain of the whip to their backs.

The White man wanted the African slave to forget his African Heritage so it would be easier to tame the beast in the African from the Congo of Africa. The White man wanted the African slaves to except slavery wholeheartedly. But what the Whites really were trying to show and tell the Africans was that they believed, whole heartedly, that Whites were the Most Supreme Race on Planet Earth.

The slaves consisted of, men, women, boys and girls. They would be marched out to the auction blocks and put on display like cattle. They would either be butt naked or just covered by a small cloth over their genitalia. Then the White slave owners would come out to Gaulke over the slaves and bid on them until they were satisfied with what they came for. Even White female slave owners were there bidding on the slaves for their own plantations. The White women were especially interested in the Big Black Bucks.

They needed them to breed with their young slave wenches. And at certain times, the female slave owners would secretly, late at night, have the bucks come to their bedside and take care of them sexually. If the White men found this to be true, that slave would be hung or maybe tar and feathered.

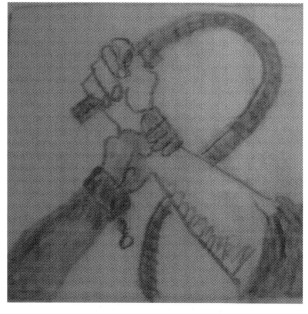 Jacob was a big dreamer and he hated to see his fellow

Africans treated in a bad way because of the hatred that the White man showed Blacks in America. His favorite daydream was to see one day that Blacks would one day rise up in unity and stop slavery altogether and for All men to be Free. He felt that All men should be treated equal as God the Father created us to be. But he lived in a time period that all people did not feel the same way. White people from the Southern States were taught that all Black Negros were always going to be inferior to White people, man or woman. No matter what President Lincoln would later say about all men are created equal. Most Southern Whites loved slavery and hated Blacks. Some Whites even believed that Negros were related to Monkeys or Apes. Some even thought that African Blacks had tails.

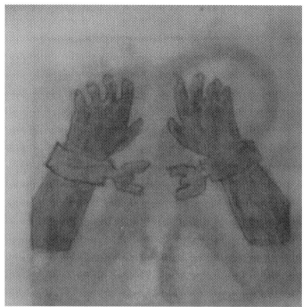

Jacob would dream of the day that the African slaves break out of the shackles and chains of slavery and just live like free men and women. Jacob would stand by his Massa's side as his Massa, bid on and bought new African women to breed and become slaves on the Jackson plantation. He remembered when he stood on the very same auction blocks when his Massa bid on him years ago. Jacob thought to himself, how time flies, even when he was not having fun. How is it fun being owned by someone that enslaves you?

After Jacob's Massa had finished his business, they gathered up his new slaves and put them in the buckboard and proceeded to return to the plantation. As Jacob approached a certain area where a lot of slaves were hung, he saw an unforgettable site. This is the place where slaves were hung. It seemed like every week or weekend some slave or slaves were being hung on this very tree. The Whites would leave the hung slaves there for days to show the rest of the slaves what could happen to them. Especially slaves that tried to escape or didn't follow the White man's rules.

As he got closer to this small hill, he saw the silhouetteof a slave that had been hung on the left side of this big tree and on the right side of the tree was a little White girl swinging nonchalantly from this same tree, with not a care in the world. What a site for a slave to see. He always thought that his bad dreams and the bad images would never stop. Jacob had very bad nightmares after coming to America and seeing what the Whites were all about and he wondered all the time, what was the big deal about being called a nigger since he got to the States?

He thought that they called him a nigger because Africans from Nigeria were called niggers because they come from the land of Nigeria. In Africa, Nigerians were always known as niggers. So, to Jacob, it was an honor to be called a nigger. Jacob hated certain images of slavery, because he could not control the recurring nightmares he endured since being captured by the slavers in Africa and being forced to come to America just to become a slave.

Jacob and Sarah, yearned to be free, but like most slaves they were under the yoke of the master's whip. The plantation owners laid down the law years ago about slaves and they would control the life of their slaves 100% of their lives. Jacob and Sarah was a lucky couple as the plantation owner took a shine to the both of them. So, every night before bed he would thank the Lord God for his and Sarah's blessings. At one time, Jacob thought about running away to fight in the Civil War on the side of the Union Soldiers up North. But every time he thought that thought, he dismantled that thought really quick, fast and in a hurry. Jacob was no fool, as he waited for his time to escape the plantation.

He wanted to find that Underground Railroad. The outbreak of the Civil War forever changed the future of the American nation. The war began as a struggle to preserve the Union, not a struggle to free the slaves, but many in the North and South felt that the conflict would ultimately decide both issues.

Many slaves escaped to the North in the early years of the war, and several Union generals established abolitionist policies in the Southern land that they conquered. Time and again some plantation owners would visit another plantation and buy a slave or two from other plantation owners and this one-day Jacob watched as two strangers rode onto the plantation to attempt to buy a couple slaves from Massa Jackson. He would always shake and shiver because he seen so many slaves get divided by the Massa and sold to other slave owners.

His Massa would sell the son or daughter of one of his slaves without hesitation. He was very thankful when the strangers would leave because that meant that he would not lose Sarah and their future children, to the vermin that trafficked in human cargo. These Southern Whites bought slaves as easy as buying groceries. Some days while driving the buckboard, Jacob wondered what it would be like to just keep on driving across the Mississippi border. He wanted to see Arkansas and Alabama. He also wanted to go further east and see Georgia and the Carolinas.

He often thought about seeing Florida's Coast, once again and again, seeing the Atlantic Ocean. But what he really wanted to see was what the North looked like, and he wondered how Blacks were treated in the Northern cities. He longed to know the answers to these questions but was very afraid to find out for himself. He was tired of seeing the hatred and turmoil that was going on in the plantations all over Mississippi.

Jacob knew what he could lose if he got caught trying to run away with his wench. They had watchmen and slave catchers all over the land. He could not take the chance of escaping his oppressors with Sarah by his side. He knew if they ever got caught attempting such an act, it would mean certain death.

Jacob would daydream about all kinds of things that were going on in his life. Most of the time he would reflect back on his trip to the Americas.

He wondered what kind of man would treat other humans the way that the slavers treated his African brothers and sisters. He watched

African men and women get hung and raped, divided from their children and men get thrown overboard when they got sick. He was even whipped just for looking at a White woman, that just happened to be on that slave ship that day and he was almost hung about that situation.

He was in a whole new world from the one he had just come from and he knew that this strange and violent world was not going to be healthful to him or his kind. These times were really trying for Jacob as he longed to be back with his friends and family. He really missed his homeland of Africa and now he felt the appreciation of growing up there. As he watched the coast disappear, he felt in his heart that he would never see Mother Africa again. It was a long and grueling trip from the Ivory Coast of Africa to the sandy Coast of Florida. His captors would keep the Africans shackled like animals, so he felt trapped on the slave ship with no way to escape.

Most Africans could not swim and to jump off the ship shackled the way they were, it was impossible to get away without drowning. So, Jacob got caught in his own back yard and he knew he was going to pay for it the rest of his life, whether it would be short or long. But he would do what he could to survive. One day after a few days of sailing and seeing how the slavers were going to treat the Africans, some of the African leaders began to talk to each other.

They conspired to overtake the whites who they called Too bob and take over the ship and make some of the Too bob turn the ship around and go back to Africa. So, when they were let out of the hold this one day, on a given signal the slaves were free of their shackles and hurriedly overtook a couple of the slavers that were on watch. The Africans actually was able to get a aboard a skiff that was trailing the slave ship. They even got the mast up to begin the journey back to the Ivory Coast.

They even killed a few of the White sailors but then, they were quickly overtaken themselves, by pistol and cannon fire. It was a monumental move, but about fifty Africans lost their lives trying to escape the enemy, who they called the Too bob.

Again, Jacob watched his fellow kinsmen lose life and limb trying to escape their oppressors. He prayed to his God for his and the other African's safety and good health.

 These revolts happened a lot out at sea when the Africans became desperate to get away and out of danger. They just wanted to go back to where they came from.

Sometimes Jacob wished that he would've gone down with his fellow man and later he found himself thanking God for still being alive. It was a lot of storms out to sea that month so a lot of the captured got seasick. They had never been out to sea or over the Ocean before. Living conditions down in the hold was filthy and it stayed that way all the way to America. Some Africans got so sick they caught diseases and were thrown overboard.

When they finally reached their destination, they were put in stocks and forced to march to the auction blocks. Some went to the Carolinas, some went to Virginia, and some were spread out to Georgia, Mississippi, Kentucky, Tennessee and Louisiana also Missouri, and Arkansas. Some even went all the way to Kansas. Jacob would end up on the Jackson Plantation in Laurel, Mississippi. It was here that his name was changed from Shaka Aki Abu to Jacob and Jackson for the last name from his soon to be Massa.

Jacob was still a teenager about nineteen years old but wiser than most his age. He learned really quick about the ways of the Whites from Mississippi. He noticed that some Whites were good, and some were not so good to Blacks, especially to Africans. The White man had come from Europe as Pilgrims and was befriended by the Native Indians. They had their first big feast with these Indians and traded different merchandise with them in the winter of 1620.

They also were taught a lot of information on how to survive thru the harsh American winters. The Indians also taught the Pilgrims how to plant corn called maze and how to plant other crops. The Africans soon found out that the Whites in America had even took over the native Indian's lands and enslaved some of them with some of the Mexican Race also being enslaved.

In some instances, they had even enslaved some of their own White Race. Jacob would further wonder, why enslave the indigenous people of that day when they helped save the lives of so many White Pilgrims. The American Indians were Flimflammed and Hoodwinked. The Pilgrims had landed on Plymouth Rock, but Plymouth Rock had landed on the Indians. What a betrayal.

History has it that the White man forced every tribe of American Indian off their lands and killed millions of them if they didn't live on a reservation. Many brave Indians resisted this treaty and fought against, who they called the White Eyes, their favorite name for the White man. Jacob thought even to be on a reservation, governing your own self, and people, would be better than being a slave working on a plantation for someone else without reward or pay.

As Jacob was getting settled into his new environment on the Jackson plantation he watched as the overseer brought new horses to the stables. They were spooked by all the hustle and bustle of the slaves going to and fro singing and working. The overseer was having a very hard time controlling these horses. Jacob volunteered his services to help harness the horses and calm them down. The overseer found that Jacob loved managing the livestock, so the overseer made him a deal.

If Jacob could be trustworthy enough to handle the animals without harm to them, he would make him a manager over all the livestock. Jacob agreed and helped put the horses safely in the stables. He was to become a pretty good animal handler. Jacob agreed to the overseer's demands and became the number one animal handler of the plantation. He would soon be the most trustworthy slave on the Jackson plantation.

Every day after that, Jacob would wake up to feed and water his animals. He would care for the newborns and helped nurture them. He would also train the horses and exercise them all day long. Then he would pick one and just ride around the plantation watching the field slaves sing and toil in the cotton, tobacco and sugar cane fields. A lot of the field slaves were very jealous of Jacob, so he kept to himself.

One fine morning Jacob was watering the horses when he saw an old man sitting in the yard playing a musical instrument that he had never seen or heard before. He slowly approached the man and introduced himself. As the man

shook Jacob's hand, he told him his name was
Abraham, but everybody called him Abe or
Old Abe. Jacob quickly told Abe that his music
sounded good and that he liked to hear more.
He did not know the name of the instrument
Abe was playing so he asked him for the name
of it. Abe told Jacob that it was a harmonica.

Jacob
loved the sound of that harmonica and would
listen to Abe play it all the live long day for
many days to come. They grew to be very close

friends. Abe told Jacob one day that he should let him mentor him and show him how to play the instrument.

Jacob agreed and took daily lessons from the Old African Musician. They both enjoyed their time together and before Abe died, he had taught the younger African many worldly things about slavery and plantation life. Jacob learned after Abe's death he had been bequeathed the harmonica that he was so fond of.

Jacob would then sit under a sycamore tree that was on the plantation and play that harmonica and cry in remembrance of Abe. He would sometimes play Abe's favorite songs and just remember what he learned from the Old Coot.

Then one day the Massa of the plantation came down from the big house to talk with Jacob. He told him how proud he was on hearing how good he was handling his livestock and wanted to explain to Jacob a new position he had planned for him.

The Massa wanted Jacob to become his new carriage driver and that he would be moving into the carriage house that was alongside the big house as soon as possible. Jacob could not believe his ears when the Massa spoke to him this way. That was one of the happiest days Jacob had since coming to the Jackson plantation. He agreed and accepted this newfound position and transitioned beautifully from livestock manager to carriage driver.

So, he moved all his possessions into his new living quarters and when the Massa seen his tattered clothes, he told Jacob he needed to get him a whole new wardrobe. So, they rode into town and bought the new wardrobe fit for a carriage driver. Jacob was the talk of the town. All around the plantation he walked and carried himself like the cock of the yard, to the point that half of the female winches started eyeing him in a different light. And most of the men slaves didn't like that one bit.

Some days Jacob would drive the Massa and his wife to town for social gatherings and he would stay with the carriage and tend to the horses while his Massa and wife had a good time dancing, drinking and associating with their fellow neighbors. This would only happen a couple times a year, but Jacob liked it when he could visit other places outside the plantation. Just to get away from that devilish place would give him joy and time to daydream about escaping to the North.

He really wanted to see what the Northern States were all about. He wanted to see and feel the environment of the North. He would even sometimes dream about being an officer in the Union Army and help the North Emancipate his fellow African brethren. He felt that he and the other slaves would never be free but that did not stop him from having his daydreams about the subject. Jacob yearned to be free and promised himself that one day it would be true.

Now it was coming to the day and time for the auctions to begin in the town, so the Massa one day told Jacob to get the carriage ready and bring it up to the big house.

They both drove to town where this time instead of staying with the horses and the carriage the Massa told Jacob to join him at the auction blocks.

Jacob was distraught at the site of these newfound Africans just landing in America for the first time being scared to death of what was happening to them. The slaves were made to stand on the blocks and stripped of their clothes while the White Plantation owners, men and women, looked at their teeth, genitals and even spread the African's butt cheeks apart while just clawing over them and their bodies. Jacob saw all of this and he felt shame and embarrassment for the slaves and for himself.

He hated his memories of those days. He remembered when it was time for his Massa to pick out some slave wenches and he told Jacob to choose one for himself. Jacob could not believe his ears. He would have the chance to save one poor would be slave for himself. So, he chose a beautiful golden brown sista who looked frightened by all that was happening. But in his old African language he communicated with her. That, for the time being would ease her mind. This was one memory that he liked. They both would later find out that she came from the same African Village that Jacob was taken from.

After the Massa ended his bidding they quietly drove back to the plantation with the new slaves. The slaves went to the slave quarters and Jacob and his women went into their home. The next day the Massa visited Jacob and told him that he would let him name his wench, so Jacob named her Sarah.

Her name was Asabe Manu in African. Sarah saw how the other slaves were living and hated white oppression just as much as Jacob did and quickly learned the ways of the White overseers and plantation owners. She prayed for relief every day after that and did what she could do to help her fellow slaves. Jacob and Sarah had been together for about three months when they decided they were ready to jump the broom. So, one Saturday afternoon they had permission from the Massa to have a wedding and invite all the slaves on the plantation since it was a wedding day, they had only to work half a day.

They had a nice wedding and danced all night long. Jacob even played his harmonica. The Massa's wife even let her cook bake the wedding cake and other fixings, while the slave wenches all pitched in and did a potluck type of dinner. Everyone had loads of fun at the reception. Even the Massa and his wife showed up for a short time. They wanted to wish the newlyweds good tidings of joy. Jacob and his new bride were very thankful for this night, so they made a toast of thanks to the Massa and his wife before they went back to the big house. They were kind and generous Southern folks. Jacob and Sarah also thanked the rest of the slaves for coming out to their reception and then they all retired to their homes.

In the days and months to come the newly wedded Jackson couple would make a big announcement that Sarah was pregnant and expecting to have their first child. Every one that heard the news was excited for the couple and some of the older women started knitting sweaters and blankets for the soon to be mother. Jacob was so proud he could not stop smiling and telling whoever would listen about his blessings. First a prestigious job, then a pretty wife and now a brand-new baby. He longed for a son of his own to teach the ways of his African Heritage. Even if he had to give him an American name, Jacob told Sarah that no matter what they have, boy or girl, they would be taught African Culture. Their child was to be born of African blood so that would make the child an African American Slave.

In anticipation of the arrival of this newborn the couple fixed up the extra back room of the carriage house with colorful trinkets, balloons and Jacob even bought a bassinette with some of his earnings from driving. Everything was looking up to be a spectacular blessing for the two star struck lovers. Then one day Jacob announced that in his country it was a special time. It was time for All Africans to celebrate just being African and also to just celebrate their country of Africa period. So, it was a special day for Jacob and Sarah. But again, they had to get permission from the Massa and once again he was generous enough to let them party that day on into the late evening.

They roasted a pig and cooked all kinds of different African culinary dishes. They displayed African masks and ornaments. They sang African songs in African and did African dances. Everyone had a lovely time. It was so nice to have a Massa that understood how important it was to these African slaves to celebrate their Heritage. Then they all sat down to feast and held hands in a circle while one of the Elders said a prayer in thanks for all the bounty they were about to receive. The Slaves were very, very thankful for what the Lord had given them on this day of celebration. As the sun set, they gathered together to watch the sun go down. Now after the festivities were over, everyone went back to their own homes on the Plantation.

One day after sitting around the house doing nothing, the Massa's wife came out to talk with Sarah. She offered her a position in the kitchen to help her favorite cook called Mammie prepare the food. Sarah was full of joy that day and loved the idea of staying busy working in the kitchen beside Mammie. Every morning she would help fix the first family breakfast and at the same time Jacob was also invited to eat in the big house when he was not working. He would often go down to the stables and give the horses a visit and a rub down on his free time.

Jacob even felt that the horses enjoyed his routine of rubbing them down to a silky shine and then exercising them. He would bring the horses sugar cubes because it was a sweet treat that all the horses liked.

On not so fine of a day, a favorite horse of the carriage team got terribly sick to the point where the veterinarian had to come out to check on the horse. His diagnosis was not a good one. His prognosis was that it would be in the owner's best interest, to put the horse down. As the plantation owner heard the news, he told his overseer to carry out the deplorable act.

As the overseer was about to shoot the horse Jacob stopped him and begged the Massa to give the horse to him and he would nurture the horse back to health. He promised if he just had a couple of weeks and the horse wasn't better, he himself would put the horse down. So, the Massa agreed and told Jacob from that day he had two weeks only to get the horse healthy. He even promised Jacob that if the horse lived, he could have him. Jacob would pray every day for a miracle to happen and he worked feverously to do whatever he could for his favorite horse. At first the horse would not eat or drink for almost a week. It really looked bad for the horse and Jacob felt so awful that he had to watch without being able to get the horse healthy in a hurry. But Jacob would not give up on this horse and he just persisted and was very determined to save his would-be horse.

With a little help from some of the African midwives, together they force fed the horse and sooner rather than later the horse slowly got better. Jacob had a gift and it was showing compassion and love to the animals and humans on the Jackson plantation. He started to see life come back in the horse's eyes.

So, it was not a surprise to see Jacob and the horse out in the pasture exercising. While the horse was in the pasture he ate like a stud and started galloping around like a newborn pony. Jacob could finally breathe easy. The next day the Massa, overseer and the vet came down to the stalls to see what Jacob and the Midwives had accomplished and all of them were flabbergasted at the site of the beautiful specimen of a healthy horse. Now it was owned by Jacob per what his Massa had promised.

They congratulated Jacob and then went away. In no time at all, Jacob was riding on the horse all around the land. After his daily chores he would harness his horse and they would ride into the wind for hours. He got tired of calling his horse just plain horse so one day he decided to give his horse a name. Jacob came up with Tadala which means, we have been blessed in the African language. This horse was now Jacob's pride and joy.

And God knows that to be very true. The Massa and his wife were really taken with Jacob's character and they would invite him and Sarah over to the big house at times for dinner and cocktails. That was something that most slave owners didn't do. To eat and drink at the same table with a slave back in those days was a no-no in the White World. But the Jacksons were not your average White couple.

One day the Jackson's were going to handle some business matters, so they left their eight-year-old daughter with Mammie. They had done that over a thousand times before, with no problem. After leaving the plantation, security measures were enforced to the fullest. After sundown every slave would pray together before splitting up and going their separate ways. It was a hot night, and everyone was on edge.

After a while, it was heard from the slave quarters to the big house that someone was taken. Some confederate soldiers, on hard times, had kidnapped the Jackson's daughter, who at that time was about nine years old. They did it so they could get ammunition, clothing and food to help the cause to win the civil war.

After hearing about this incident, Jacob knew this was his time to shine. He had day-dreamed about being a hero all his Southern Life. And in his dreams, he would always fight against the Southern Confederate Army. That was because he hated the hateful and the prejudiced man, Black or White. That day Jacob would take his favorite horse and dog to look for his Massa's daughter. Jacob knew that he did not have a lot of time to find his Massa's daughter. He would not give up until the Massa's daughter was brought home safe and sound.

Hannah was her name and she was the Master of the plantations only child. It was common for the enemy to kidnap children or wives for collateral, but this was not the enemy but a Southern AWOL group of Rebels trying to gain leverage to get a ransom to buy more weapons to fight against the Northern Armies. A group of men from the South, joined Jacob and the Massa would also help look for the little girl. They teamed up to fight against the Southern rebellion.

They took the hound dogs out and the dogs quickly picked up Hannah's scent. Jacob led the charge that evening and that night, they came upon a camp just beyond this ridge. Jacob charged this one tent and found Hannah tied to a steak. He silently untied her, and they left thru a slit that he had cut in the back of the tent. Soon the rebels woke up and a fight ensued.

The rebels were quickly destroyed, and Hannah was brought back to the Jackson

Plantation in good spirits thanks to Jacob and the rest of the Southern rebellion fighters. The Jacksons were very grateful to all who had helped bring their baby girl back home. But he really wanted to thank Jacob personally. He told Jacob that he had a special reward for him because of his loyalty and dedication of service. He eventually told Jacob that he would give him and his wife Sarah their freedom plus a plot of land in the back forty after five more dedicated years of service. Jacob agreed to this proposition and dreamed of the day that He and Sarah could raise a family while living as free African Americans.

Then one day the American President, who was Abraham Lincoln made the Emancipation Proclamation Speech in which he believed that all men were and are created equal. That Emancipation would free the slaves. That disturbed the White Southerners so much that they wanted to start a war to keep the Ante Bellum South exactly the way it was born. They wanted to keep slavery in the Deep South

Active. The Northern folks of the Union stated, "we will go to war with you over your decision" and that started the War Between the States, also known as the war between the North and South. We know it today as the Civil War.

A few months went by and the Civil War was going on at a nice clip. The cannon blasts and sounds of war were getting closer and closer to the Jackson plantation. One day a couple of Confederate soldiers rode onto the plantation and asked for the owner of the property. The overseer and Mr. Jackson soon arrived at the front gate to see what the problem was. The soldiers told Mr. Jackson that their army would be coming to the plantation for provisions and they would take what they needed with or without the say so from the plantation owner.

Every day the slaves were forced to support the confederate army in some way or another. They would be told to help with food, water, clothing and helptaking care of the horses of the confederates. Some slaves resisted and were whipped, so, some ran away. Other slaves were even attacked in the night and some wenches were raped. Some of the slaves that could not find the Underground Railroad joined a rebellion.

One of the leaders of the revolt and or rebellion was a slave called Nat Turner.

Nat Turner's Revolt was a slave rebellion that took place in Southampton County, Virginia, in August 1831, led by Nathanial Turner. Rebel slaves killed from 55 to 65 people, at least 51 being white. The rebellion was put down within a few days, but Turner survived in hiding for more than two months afterwards. The rebellion was effectively suppressed at Belmont Plantation on the morning of August 23, 1831.

Jacob and Sarah did not like it when these confederate soldiers would stop by the plantation. He had to be very aware of the safety of the plantation because these men were just taking what they wanted at will. Massa Jackson did not like it either but was not at liberty to fight them off without collateral damage to his own family. They would have to endure the vicious treatment of these soldiers until sometime in the future they would depart from the Jackson plantation.

So, the slaves and their Massa had to obey the commands and demands of the confederate army officers, until they parted for duty. This action went on for weeks with Jacob and the Massa going into town to get supplies for the army and Mammie and Sarah spent all day in the kitchen cooking for the soldiers. While all this was happening, the Massa's wife spent her days patching up the wounded.

Then one day, just like that the army thanked the Jacksons for their hospitality and left to go fight against the Union Army. It was a big relief when it was all over, soon enough the plantation went back to full steam ahead, and every slave was at ease once again working in the fields.

Once again, the Southern Confederate Army was out in the lands of Mississippi fighting against the Union Soldiers from the North and again kayos soon followed. The Union Soldiers were winning the war and were constantly pushing back the Southerners. Now the slaves on the Jackson plantation feared that very soon they would again be greeted with more visitors. Next time it would be from the Union Soldiers.

And so, it was one balmy day when the slaves were coming in from the fields that they noticed soldiers approaching the plantation. Jacob was caring for the horses when he and the overseer also witnessed the large Calvary coming thru the gate of the Jacksons land. The Captain of the guard hurriedly asked for the owner and explained what he wanted. It was just like the Confederate Army back for seconds.

Again, all the families, slaves and owners had to work double time to cater to this second Army. The soldiers took over the plantation for a couple of weeks. During that time, tensions ran rampant between the slaves, the owners' Jackson family members, and Jacob running errands, with Sarah and Mammie doing all the cooking.

But when the Union Soldiers left, they paid with Union Monies for what they received and thanked the Southern family. When that Army left, the anxiety of their visit left with them. Again, everyone settled down and went back to the way it was before the soldiers arrived. Even though they were still under the yoke of slavery, they felt very blessed to be alive and well.

Now after the Civil War was over, the slaves had to deal with the reconstruction of the South and learn to deal with a new danger that arrived to the South. That danger was the Carpetbaggers and Scalawags. Carpetbaggers were people that had moved to the South from the Northern States to take advantage of the people of the crippled Southern States. Usually they were in a political party. A Scalawag was a term for a Southern Republican or supporter of Reconstruction. They were viewed as traitors of the South. They were both Black and White.

Countless Carpetbaggers flocked to the South to exert a significant influence. They wanted to Modernize and Republicanize the Old South into the New South. They eventually were driven out by the Democratic State Politicians in the mid-1870s.

There was some resistance to reconstruction in the New South. Most White Southerners did not want Blacks to be equal. Most landowners refused to rent property to Blacks. So, violence to Blacks, Carpetbaggers and Scalawags was common. Some of the Southerners hated that President Lincoln wanted to free all of the slaves so they conspired to kill him.

They elected John Wilkes Booth to shoot the President while attending a Play. Booth snuck in behind Mr. Lincoln, who was sitting by his wife in the balcony seats of the Ford Theater and shot the President in the back of the head, then Booth jumped down from that balcony and broke one of his legs.

He then ran and jumped on a horse and rode off from Washington <u>DC</u> and was found in a barn sometimes in Virginia, twelve days later.

Lincoln did not die right away. Many doctors were called to his bedside to diagnose his condition, but the prognosis was the same between all of them. His condition was considered hopeless. He lingered for a while and eventually he died. The ex-slaves cried when they heard this sad news. They loved President Lincoln. And they would miss him and his patriotism.

Now after the assassination of President Lincoln the slaves were enjoying their freedom and the ex-slaves had parties happening all over the South. Eventually some would stay with the Massa of their plantations and some would travel up North to look for work. Then others would go further north to Canada. All the White Southerners did not like to see the Negroes leave.

They knew they would be losing free labor, which meant less profits and monetary gain. So again, a conspiracy of the White man began to scare and terrorize the Negro to go back to the old ways of the South and forget about being and living free. This is when the Ku-Klux-Klan was born. They were also known as the KKK, White Supremacist's born out of hatred of the Negro, the Africans and all African Americans. They hated any race of people not White like them. Especially Africans, African Americans,

Indians, Mexicans and Jewish people known as Jews. They were not fond of Asians either, like Chinese and Japanese people.

From the late 1860s white supremacists in the KKK (Ku Klux Klan) terrorized African American leaders and citizens in the South until, in 1871, the US Congress passed legislation that resulted in the arrest and imprisonment of Klan leaders and the end of the Klan's terrorism of Americans for a time. By this time Jacob and Sarah was given a new home in the back forty by his ex-Massa Mr. Jackson per his promise years ago.

They were also given horses, chickens, mules and some dairy cows with one bull to stud. Jacob would not hesitate to plant his own crops of sugar cane and tobacco. He did not and would not ever grow cotton for that was the commodity that most slaves had to pick. It was also associated with White wealth. He would profit from other crops and his business of running and owning a livery stable.

When the Klan heard about any Negroes owning any land, property or a business, they would come around and try to rain terror on those Negroes. The Klan would come out late at night when it got dark wearing white hoods over their face, so no one knew who they were.

They would burn Negros's houses, break their windows, take the cattle, steal the children and anything they could do to deter the Negros from advancing financially. Jacob and his family would often get these visits also. The KKK would come by his livery stable and would threaten him, using his family as bait. But Jacob was a strong African and he would do whatever it took to protect his friends and family.

Then one day Jacob heard that the Klan had hung a few of his friends that were freed from the Jackson plantation and the Klan had even raped their wives and daughters. The Klan then came around that next night and burned all the sugarcane and tobacco fields that belonged to Black folks. Negroes from all over Mississippi came to Laurel to help the ex-slaves fight the KKK. It was time to start fighting back, especially for the children. No matter what the Negroes did to prevent the KKK from terrorizing the Southern territory, it did not work.

Because of the Black resistance, the Klan started burning down and blowing up Negro churches all over the South. They harmed and killed thousands of Negros and the city sheriffs and judges did nothing to help because they had white hoods also. Some of the Africans would gather together and talk about Black unity because they realized they had strength in numbers. But some of them thought that they were better off when they were slaves. "At least we were taken care of and didn't have to worry about these kinds of terrorists" some would say out loud. But most Blacks just wanted to be totally free from the oppression of the Whites.

Jacob then noticed that as the Civil War came to a close, southern states began to pass a series of state laws known as the Black codes. These laws were designed to keep the Whites supreme over the Negro. It also helped define White Supremacy. The codes even stopped Blacks from voting and serving on juries. In some states, these rights varied. They didn't even have the right to own or carry any type of weapons or lease or rent land, let alone own some land. It was true that White plantation owners relied on slavery for economic stability in the South before the war; now, black codes ensured that same stability. Blacks were forced to work for many plantation owners for free.

Any former slaves that attempted to violate or evade this law were fined, beaten, or arrested. Upon arrest, many "free" African Americans were made to work for free, essentially being reduced to the very definition of a slave. Although slavery had been outlawed by the Thirteenth Amendment, it effectively continued in many southern states. Despite the Civil Rights Act of 1866 and Civil War Amendments and the fact that black codes were formally outlawed, Whites continued their abuse on Negros. Support for Reconstruction policies slowed down after the early 1870s, because of the violence of white supremacist organizations such as the Ku Klux Klan.

Reconstruction ended in 1877, and the freed Black people had seen little to no improvement in their economic and social status. These Black codes, from the post-Civil War era until 1968 were meant to return Southern states to an antebellum class. These laws existed for 100 years, from the post-Civil War era until 1968, as they meant to return the South to an antebellum class structure by belittling black Americans.

Negro communities and individuals that attempted to defy Jim Crow laws often met with violence and death. The roots of Jim Crow laws began as early as 1865. Black codes were strict laws detailing when, where and how freed slaves could work, and for how much compensation Blacks would and could receive.

The codes appeared throughout the South as a legal way to take voting rights away, to control where Blacks lived and how they traveled and to seize children for labor purposes. The legal system was stacked against black citizens, with ex-Confederate soldiers working as police and judges, making it difficult for African Americans to win court cases. These codes worked with labor camps for the incarcerated, where prisoners were treated as slaves.

Black offenders typically received longer sentences than their white equals, and because of the grueling work, often did not live out their entire sentence. Violence was on the rise, making danger a regular aspect of black lives. Black schools were vandalized and destroyed. Violent white folks attacked black citizens in the night.

These were sometimes gruesome incidents where the victims were tortured and mutilated before being murdered by hangings, plus tar and feathering. Sometimes they would boil a Black man in oil for having a sexual relationship with a White Woman. Families were attacked and forced off their land all across the South. The most ruthless organization of the Jim Crow era, the Ku Klux Klan, was born in 1865 in Pulaski, Tennessee as a private club for Confederate veterans. The Klan also known as the KKK, grew into a secret society terrorizing Black communities and seeping through White southern culture, with members at the highest levels of government.

At the start of the 1880s, big cities in the south were not wholly beholden to Jim Crow laws and Black Americans found more leeway in them. This led to substantial Black populations moving into the cities and, as the decade progressed, white city dwellers demanded more laws to limit opportunities for African Americans. Jim Crow laws spread around the south with even more force than previously. Public parks were forbidden for African Americans to enter, and schools, theaters and restaurants were also segregated.

One day the Whites started fighting with a Negro just minding his own business and a group of Blacks took up sticks and stones and fought the Whites off. A handful of Whites were killed, and a couple of Blacks were killed also, but the Negros had had enough. They felt like if you want to fight heads up then let's do it. Jacob was also there joining in the Frey and he was sliced across his forehead. And another one of his African brothers was killed. He was just too tired of the violence that was breaking out all across the South.

He again daydreamed about moving up North just to get away from all the hatred of the Southern Whites. Suddenly, here come the Sheriffs police to arrest all the Negros for assault and battery of Whites. Some were even charged with murder. Not one White man was taken to jail. But that was the way of the Southern White Man. If they couldn't get you one way, they would get you another way. Now Jacob and his friends were in another fight for their lives provoked by the KKK and other Whites that disliked the Negro.

The Blacks were all taken to jail and had no lawyers defending them because not one Southern lawyer wanted anything to do with defending Africans. Jacob and the others could just sit in jail and rot for all they cared. They didn't have White privilege. There was a double standard between Blacks and Whites and the Negros seen that really quick.

When Sarah heard the news, she spread the news to Mr. Jackson to see if he could help out. Mr. Jackson even went to court and spoke in behalf of Jacob and some of the other Negros but to no avail. Plus, the judge would not even let him bail Jacob out. Jacob just sat in jail and thought how the Judge probably, secretly wore his white hood and robe in Cognito.

Jacob did not trust any official of the government to give a Black man an honest break. So, he just sat in his cell in constant doom. His life did not mean a thing to these White Southern prejudice folks. He felt like he was lost in a sea of White Southern Supremacy. But Jacob was a proud African and he would not bow down to any White man no matter what land he lived in.

It looked like Jacob and his friends were going to be convicted of a crime that was incited by the Whites from town. The Negros could only sit in court and listen to lie after lie. The judge and the All-White jury would not even believe a word that the Africans were saying. The Blacks did not even get a chance to defend themselves because they were never called up to the witness stand. Jacob and his friends were convicted and were sentenced to be hung.

All they could do is pray after the verdict was in. Mr. Jackson and Sarah could not believe their eyes and ears when they heard the guilty verdict on all counts for all of the African slaves. Jacob would not even be able to see his child being born. He thought that God had let him down and had abandoned him. The judge let

Sarah hug and kiss Jacob for the last time and he also let Mr. Jackson talk to Jacob for the last time. After that, the Negros were given their last meal and led to the gallows or to the nearest tree to be hung. Jacob thought to himself, all that had happened to him that was good was now going to be taken from him. He would lose his business. He would lose his friends. He would lose his wife and unborn child. He would lose his lifestyle, but most of all he would lose his life.

The time of the end for Jacob had finally arrived and the Grim Reaper was knocking at his door and it was wide open for him to step in. Jacob had finally lost all hope of being a free man ever again.

And the Reaper never hesitates to take a life when the time comes. So, Jacob said his last prayer to the Lord in the name of Jesus. His last daydream was about him and his family being free and wealthy, living up North and making enough money to go back to Africa with his children.

Jacob woke this fine day with Sarah shaking him from his deep sleep and his son and daughter jumping up and down from the bed to his chest.

He was home in his own bed with the family that he loved.

He looked out his bedroom window to see his livestock up and at it, eating in one of the fields that he had been given as a reward. Living that is and enjoying the lush green grass and hay from the pasture. He finally woke from a Terrible Dream. He hugged his children and put a long sweet kiss on the lips of his wife Sarah.

Then he thanked the Lord Thy God for all his blessings. After all the things that had happened to him, he woke up into reality. He had just realized that he owned the forty acres that His Massa once promised him, free and clear.

He was his own Master now and he also took a handful of slaves from his old plantation and now he let them go free also, giving them a small plot of land on his property to raise and grow their own choice of crops.

He also let them keep the profits for themselves. Jacob was a giving and compassionate man. He owned all the livestock and the crops out in the pasture in the fields. But beyond his own belief, he had earned his freedom years ago before his Massa died for saving Hannah. Now he lived as a Free Man with a family that he truly loved. He thanked God again for his self, his friends and his family's freedom.

For all that had happened to Jacob and Sarah, after he saved Hannah and was rewarded his land and his freedom was true, the rest of the latter story was him just dreaming. When Jacob and Sarah first came to the plantation, they worked in the field with the rest of the field slaves picking cotton and tobacco. They both were cotton pickers. That is how they met. Now, in real life, because he won his freedom years ago saving his master's daughter, they were really a married couple that had two children and all of them were free spirits and also, property owners.

Jacob woke up this morning and finally realized the Truth of the matter was that, it was All just a dream. Thank God, it was All just a dream.

THE END
Denson Jones

Printed in the United States
By Bookmasters